SAM'S DUCK

Written by Michael Morpurgo
Illustrated by Keith Bowen

FARMS FOR CITY CHILDREN

Nethercott is one of three farms run by the educational charity, Farms for City Children. Every year three thousand children come with their teachers to spend a week living and working on the farms. They come in all seasons, in all weathers. Now more than ever it matters that children can experience life in the countryside. Calves are born, sheep are shorn and foxes kill chickens. And this is not something the children just watch. They feed the hens, hiss at the geese and hear owls hoot in the night. They are the farmers.

Michael Morpurgo

For all the children who come to Nethercott,
Treginnis and to Wick
MM

To Jennifer
KB

First published in hardback in Great Britain by HarperCollins*Publishers* Ltd in 1996
First published in Picture Lions in 1997
1 3 5 7 9 10 8 6 4 2
ISBN: 0 00 664 625 5
Picture Lions is an imprint of the Children's Division, part of HarperCollins Publishers Ltd
Text copyright © Michael Morpurgo 1996 Illustration copyright © Keith Bowen 1996
The HarperCollins website address is: www.fireandwater.com
Printed and bound in Singapore by Imago

"YOU'LL like it when you get there," said Sam's grandad.
"I won't," said Sam. But he knew he had to go to the
farm. Everyone in Mrs Southerden's class was going. Besides,
Grandad said it would be good for him. "City boy like you can
learn a lot down on the farm," he said. "Fresh air, fresh eggs.
I wish I could go myself. You'll be back on Friday for my
birthday. We'll have a party."

Grandad waved goodbye. Sam watched from the back of the
coach till he couldn't see him anymore. It was a whole week
before he would be home again. Sam did his best not to cry.

IT was a long way to Devon. Motorways turned to roads, roads turned to lanes, narrow lanes with grass growing down the middle. Suddenly ahead of them was a huge house, like a palace, with green fields and trees all around.

"That's Nethercott," said Mrs Southerden from the front of the bus. "We're here. And what are you now?"

"Farmers!" they chorused.

AND so they were. Up with the dawn and out to work. Milking cows,

feeding horses and pigs and calves.

AND the sheep had to be fed too. All before breakfast. Breakfast was steaming porridge, scrambled eggs and all the toast you wanted.

THEN there were sheds to muck out, hens and ducks and geese to let out, eggs to collect. There was even a bull, but you weren't allowed in his field, just in case.

Sam didn't have time to miss Grandad. They worked all afternoon too and even then it wasn't finished. In the evening the cows had to be milked again – and do cows make a mess!

The lambing sheep were brought into the barns for the night, the pigs fed, the horses groomed and the hens and ducks and geese shut up in case the fox came skulking up the lane.

SAM worked like a Trojan, ate like a king and slept like a log. The farmers were kind and smiling, especially the old gardener who brought the vegetables to the kitchen. He had silver hair like Sam's Grandad.

SAM loved every minute of it. Even when they had to muck out stinky sheds or clear a field of stones so the corn could grow through in the spring.

BUT best of all was the time when he reached inside a sheep and hauled out a lamb, warm and wet and steaming in the frosty air. He watched her breathe her first breath, walk her first step, drink her first milk. He had so much to tell Grandad.

O NLY Lisa didn't enjoy it. 'Mona' Lisa, Mrs Southerden called her. "My feet hurt, Miss. My back aches, Miss. It's cold, Miss." All week she never stopped moaning.

TUESDAY was Market day. It was the first thing Sam hadn't liked. In the auction ring there was a red-faced man who twisted the calves' tails to make them move. He even kicked them, and all the time he laughed like a drain.

SAM couldn't bear to watch him. He went outside and looked at the ducks and chickens instead. They huddled together in the backs of their cages. But one of them, a lovely snowy white duck, stood by the wire and quacked at him. Sam touched his soft feathers with his finger.

"Out of my way!" It was the red-faced man. "That's my supper you're looking at." And he grabbed the duck by the feet.

"You're not going to eat him!" cried Sam. "You can't!"

"You got a better idea?" laughed the red-faced man.

Sam didn't have to think about it. "I'll buy him off you," he said, and he took out all his money. "I've got two pounds."

"It's a deal," said the red-faced man. He took the money and Sam was left cradling the duck in his arms. What was he going to do with him? What would Mrs Southerden say? Quickly, he slipped the duck into his sports bag.

"No quacking," he whispered. "*Please*!"

ALL the way home to Nethercott he wondered what to do. He walked at the back well away from the others, just in case. There was only one place he could think of to hide him; in the shed in the vegetable garden. No one would know, if he was careful, if he was lucky.

The duck stood in his shed and looked about him. He seemed to like it. "You'll need some straw for a bed," Sam told him. "And some food."

"AND water," came a voice from behind him.
It was the old gardener. "Duck's got to
have water," he said. "Where d'you get him?"

"Market," said Sam. "This man, he was
going to kill him."

"Was he now? Well, we can't have that,
can we? I've got some sandwiches in my
shed, and milk. Will that do?"

So they fed him together. "It's a drake,"
said the gardener. "We'll call him Francis,
shall we – you know, like the famous sailor –
Francis Drake?"

"No one knows I've got him," said Sam.

"I won't say a word," said the old gardener,
tapping his nose.

FOR the rest of the week the children worked hard on the farm and nobody guessed that Sam had a secret.

On the last night there was a crackling bonfire and everyone sang songs and ate too many sausages. Sam crept away to be with Francis and the old gardener. "What you going to do with him?" he asked Sam.

Sam had worked it all out. "Birthday present for my Grandad. He'll be seventy tomorrow."

"Same age as me," said the gardener. "He's a lucky man – to have a grandson like you."

NEXT morning the old gardener was waiting for him in the shed. Together they settled Francis deep down in his sports bag.

"Good luck," said the old gardener.

Sam ran for the coach, he wanted the back seat, in the corner. That was the safest place. If Francis quacked just once, that would be it. He waved goodbye to the gardener until he couldn't see him anymore.

They only stopped once. "Lunch," said Mrs Southerden. "Everyone out." Sam didn't want to leave his bag behind, but Mrs Southerden said he had to.

When he'd finished his picnic he ran all the way back to the coach. Someone was there before him. 'Mona' Lisa was bending over the back seat.

"IT quacked," she said. "You've got a duck. I'll tell."
Then Lisa was running up to the front of the bus. "Miss, Miss, Sam's got a duck in his bag."

Quickly, Sam took Francis out of his bag and hid him under his coat.

"Don't be silly, Lisa," said Mrs Southerden. "All week you've been nothing but a nuisance. And now you're telling silly tales. Come and sit at the front with the sickies, come on."

"But Miss," Lisa cried. "It's true. He's got a duck, honest."

Everyone looked at Sam. He shrugged his shoulders, sighed and held his bag up, upside down. Lisa's mouth opened and shut, just like a goldfish. Sam just smiled sweetly

But it was a very long journey home.

SAM couldn't wait to see Grandad. He ran up the steps to the flat. He made Grandad sit down with his eyes closed, while he ran a bath for Francis to paddle in. Then he called Grandad in.

"For you, Grandad," he said. "Happy birthday." And he told Grandad all about Francis and the red-faced man in the market and the old gardener down at Nethercott.

"That's a lovely, lovely duck," said Grandad, shaking his head. "But Sam, we can't keep him up here in the flat. Wouldn't be right."

"Why not?"

"Listen Sam," Grandad said. "A duck needs a pond. He needs friends too, like you, like me. And he needs his freedom."

All evening Sam tried to persuade Grandad to keep Francis. But it didn't do any good.

"We'll talk about it in the morning," said Grandad. "Get some sleep now."

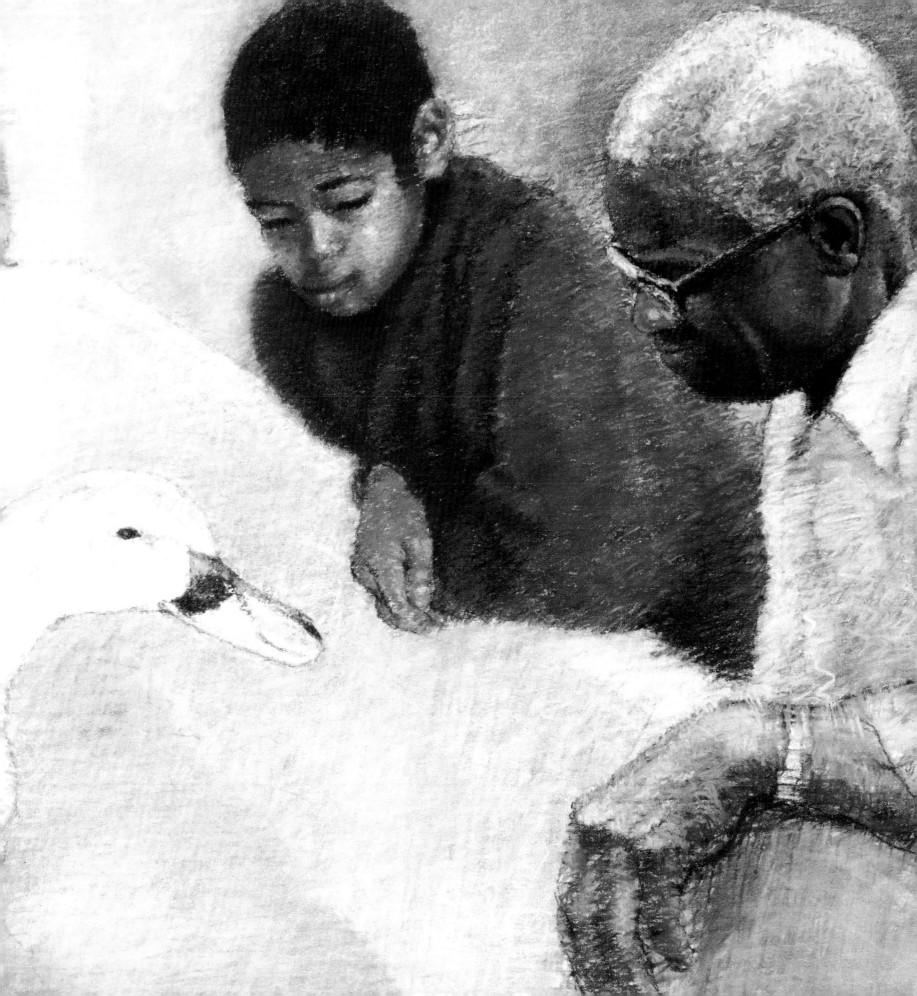

Grandad got him up early
the next morning.
"What's up?" Sam asked.
"You'll see," said Grandad.
They set off with Francis in Sam's
sports bag, his head peeking out.
There was no one else about.

"WHERE are we going?" Sam asked.

"You'll see," said Grandad, a twinkle in his eye.

They were walking through the park in the early morning mist, when Francis quacked. Suddenly there were other ducks quacking, and ahead of him Sam could see a great dark lake and ducks swimming towards them. There were geese too, and moorhens and swans.

They crouched down by the lake and let Francis go. He waddled into the water, settled himself, flapped his wings, shook his head and cruised out to join his friends.

"Well," said Grandad, "what do you think?"

"I suppose we can always come and feed him," said Sam.

"Every day if you like," said Grandad. "Look at him, Sam. That's a very happy duck and I'm a very happy man."